Lucky Dog Days

Lucky
Dog Days

JUDY DELTON

Illustrated by Alan Tiegreen

A YOUNG YEARLING BOOK

Published by
Dell Publishing
a division of
Bantam Doubleday Dell Publishing Group, Inc.
1540 Broadway
New York, New York 10036

The trademark Yearling® is registered in the U.S. Patent and Trademark Office.

The trademark Dell® is registered in the U.S. Patent and Trademark Office.

ISBN: 0-440-40063-5

Printed in the United States of America

August 1988

10 9 8

WES

For Julie:
Though you are far across the sea
You're still the whole wide world to me.

Contents

CHAPTER 1

Not Christmas

The Pee Wee Scouts scrambled out of cars. They ran into Mrs. Peters's house.

It was Tuesday. Time for a Pee Wee Scout meeting.

Mrs. Peters was smiling. She was their troop leader.

When everyone sat down, she said, "This is a special month. Does anyone know why it is special?"

"Christmas?" said Roger White.

All the Scouts laughed.

Roger's face turned red.

"Christmas is in winter," said Molly Duff.

"It's hot outside now and there are flowers," said Rachel Myers. She laughed at Roger.

"Some places have flowers at Christmas," said Mrs. Peters. "Like California and Hawaii."

"Ha," said Roger. He stuck his tongue out at Rachel.

Rachel raised her hand to tell Mrs. Peters.

"Tattletale," said Roger.

Mrs. Peters frowned. "The special thing about this month is not Christmas," she said.

"Is it March of Dimes month?" asked Rachel. "My dad says that's a good cause."

"No, but you're getting closer," said Mrs. Peters.

"I know!" said Sonny Betz. "I'll bet it is National Secretaries' month." Sonny's mother was a secretary.

Mrs. Peters shook her head.

"Is it Eat More Pork month?" asked Mary Beth Kelly. She remembered seeing some pigs on TV. And pork chops and sausages.

"Oink, oink," said Molly.

The rest of the Scouts began to snort.

"Well, I'll tell you," said Mrs. Peters. "It is Help-a-Pet month."

"I've got a pet!" called out Tracy Barnes. "I've got a gerbil."

Tracy's nose was running.

It was always running, thought Molly.

"That's a dumb pet," said Roger. "A dog is the best kind of pet."

Tracy looked like she was going to cry. "Snuffy isn't dumb," she said. "He can roll over and play dead."

"A gerbil?" said Molly. "A gerbil can't play dead!"

The Scouts who had cats for pets were chasing Roger around the room. "Dogs are not the best!" they shouted. "Cats are."

"I've got a horse," said Rachel.

Rat's knees! thought Molly. Rachel *would* have to have something bigger than anyone else.

Mrs. Peters held up her hand.

The Pee Wees knew that meant quiet.

"Dogs are good for some people," she said. "And cats and horses are good for others. And gerbils are good pets too."

She smiled at Tracy.

"My mom says house pets are dirty," said Rachel. She tossed her head. "Cats lick butter and shed on your clothes."

"My cat doesn't lick the butter," said Lisa Ronning.

"As I said," Mrs. Peters went on, "this

is Help-a-Pet month. I wondered how many of you would like to help a pet?"

All the Pee Wees raised their hands.

"What pets?" asked Roger. "My dog doesn't need help."

Rachel snickered.

"I was thinking of homeless pets," said Mrs. Peters. "Pets who have no one to love them. There are lots of pets at the animal shelter that have no homes. Maybe Troop 23 could take them for walks. Or raise money for more kennels. They are very short of space."

"Maybe we can adopt them," said Sonny Betz.

"Ho, ho," said Mary Beth. "How can we adopt a hundred dogs?"

The Scouts broke out into laughter again.

Mrs. Peters's dog Tiny ran into the room. He barked and barked.

"He likes the idea of adopting all the dogs," said Mrs. Peters. She laughed. "But we can't adopt them. We can only help them."

The Scouts cheered. It would be fun to help a pet.

For the rest of the meeting they all played Scout games.

Then they had milk and chocolate chip cookies.

They reported some good deeds they had done for others during the week.

Then everyone stood up to say the Pee Wee Scout pledge. And sing the Pee Wee Scout song.

After that it was time to go.

On her way home, Molly thought, Next week we're going to help a pet!

CHAPTER 2

Trouble with Snooks

Next Tuesday took forever to come.

The Pee Wees rode their skateboards to make the time go faster.

It was a hot, hot August.

They went swimming at the pool.

They climbed trees in the park.

Still it took a long time for Tuesday to come.

Finally it was time for the Pee Wees to meet again. They were going to the animal shelter for their meeting.

As they tumbled out of the cars at the shelter they could hear barks. And meows. They heard whines and whimpering.

"Someone is crying," said Mary Beth.

A lady came out to meet them. "I will take you on a tour," she said.

The Scouts followed the lady. Her name was Miss Penn.

"This is our cat room," she said.

Cages, cages, cages.

All around the room were cages.

In every cage was a cat.

Striped cats. White cats. Brown cats. Cats with long hair. Cats with short hair. Big cats. Little cats. Medium cats.

Every cat was crying. They wanted the Scouts to take them out. They put their paws through the bars. "Me-ow," they called. Take me home.

Miss Penn opened a cage door. She

took out a tiger cat. She put him in Molly's arms.

"Oooh!" squealed Molly. "He is so soft. I wish I could take him home."

Miss Penn handed each Scout a cat to hold.

When she gave Tracy a cat, she began to sneeze. Then her eyes started to tear. Tracy's nose started to run too. More than usual, thought Molly. Yuck.

"You must be allergic," said Mrs. Peters.

She took the cat and put it back in the cage.

The longer they were in the shelter, the more Tracy sneezed.

When they got to the dog room, the dogs barked at them. Tracy's eyes were nearly swollen shut.

"Dear me," said Mrs. Peters to Tracy. "You will have to wait in the car."

"My cousin is allergic too," said Rachel. "He has to get shots."

"Sonny is allergic," said Roger. "That's why he couldn't come today."

"That's not why he stayed home," said Tim Noon. "He didn't come because he's scared of dogs!"

"Baby," said Rachel. "Only babies are afraid of dogs."

More dogs began to bark. Arf! Arf!

"Now!" said Mrs. Peters loudly. "Miss Penn said these dogs would love to have a walk. You may each choose a dog and take it for a short walk around the shelter yard."

Molly wanted the cocker spaniel.

So did Roger.

"There are plenty of dogs to go around," Mrs. Peters said.

"Selfish," said Molly to Roger as she chose a beagle in the next cage.

Mary Beth chose a poodle.

13

Tim chose a dog that looked like a spaniel in front and a Labrador in back.

"He is a Heinz dog," said Mrs. Peters. "Fifty-seven varieties!"

Lisa chose a terrier.

And Rachel chose a St. Bernard called Snooks.

"That is a pretty big dog," said Miss Penn.

"Do you think you can handle him?" asked Mrs. Peters.

Rachel nodded. "My uncle has a Great Dane," she said. "I always take him for a walk."

"Liar!" said Molly.

Rachel made a face at Molly.

When they got outside, Molly's beagle walked at her heels.

So did Mary Beth's poodle.

Lisa's terrier ran and tugged at his leash. Lisa pulled him toward her.

But when Snooks got to the door, he took off like a bullet. He ran toward a little pond and he pulled Rachel with him.

"Help!" shouted Rachel as she flew past the girls.

The other dogs saw Snooks and they began to run too.

They each pulled a Scout along behind them.

Tim's Heinz dog got so excited that he ran around Tim in circles. He wrapped the leash around Tim's legs.

"Hey," called Tim. "I'm all tied up!"

Soon all the dogs were racing toward the pond behind Snooks. They pulled the Pee Wees behind them, all except Tim. He was on the ground. He tried to get unwound.

The dogs ran amuck.

The Scouts were yelling and shouting.
"Let go of the leash!" called Roger.
Everyone did.
Everyone but Rachel.

16

CHAPTER **3**

Soaked!

"**S**plash!" went Snooks into the pond. "Splash!" went Rachel right after him. Tim finally got his legs free.

Roger and Tim ran to the pond. They grabbed Rachel's arms and pulled her out. She was dripping wet and she had a water lily on top of her head.

Molly and Lisa and Mary Beth got there next. Then Mrs. Peters and Miss Penn.

"I thought you said you walked a Great Dane!" said Roger.

17

Miss Penn went back to the shelter and got a towel. She wrapped the towel around Rachel.

"My new shorts!" moaned Rachel. "They're ruined."

All of a sudden Molly began to laugh. Rachel looked so funny dripping wet.

18

With a water lily on her head.

And her clothes soaked.

Roger and Tim and Lisa and Mary Beth began to laugh too. The other Scouts joined in.

When Miss Penn and Mrs. Peters saw that Rachel was all right, they laughed too.

Roger ran off to catch Snooks.

Snooks thought he was playing. When Roger got close to him, Snooks ran. He looked like he was smiling. At last Roger caught him.

Arf! Arf! Snooks barked loudly.

The rest of the dogs had jumped into the pond and were swimming around. Then they came out, dripping wet.

Roger and Tim rounded up all the dogs.

"They needed the exercise," said Miss Penn, laughing.

"Well I didn't," said Rachel, pouting. "I don't want to help a pet anymore."

"Instead of Rachel walking a dog," said Lisa, "a dog walked Rachel!"

Rachel was still wrapped in the towel. She went to sit in the car with Tracy.

Soon everyone began to calm down. They gave the dogs a short walk. Molly tried to teach the beagle to sit up. Tim played fetch with his mutt.

"I think we have had enough for one day," said Mrs. Peters. "It's time to leave."

When the Scouts got back to Mrs. Peters's house, they drew pictures of the pets they had helped.

Molly's beagle had a red collar.

Mary Beth's dog looked like he had a plate on his head. "That's his topknot!"

said Mary Beth. "Poodles have topknots and pom-poms."

"Ho, ho," Roger laughed. "It looks like a hat."

Roger held his picture up. It was a picture of a pond. In the pond was a girl with a lily on her head.

The girl was Rachel.

"It's not funny!" shouted Rachel. "You tear that up, Roger White, or I'll tell my mother."

She began to chase Roger.

Roger held the paper over his head.

Mrs. Peters had to clap her hands.

The room grew quiet.

"Scouts," she said. "I have thought of a way to earn money to help a pet. We will have a rummage sale. Ask your mothers and fathers if they have anything to donate. Ask your neighbors too."

*　　*　　*

22

Troop 23 sang their Scout song.

Then they said the Pee Wee Scout pledge.

Time to go home, thought Molly.

She was tired.

Help-a-Pet month was hard work.

CHAPTER 4

Diamond Rummage

On Saturday morning, Tracy dialed Molly's phone number. "Let's go collect rummage today," she said.

Even over the phone Molly could tell that Tracy's nose was running.

"I'm going with Mary Beth," said Molly.

"I'll come too," said Tracy, hanging up.

"Rat's knees!" said Molly. She stamped her foot. She didn't want to go with Tracy.

24

Tracy was bossy. And she was always sniffling.

It made Molly sick to her stomach.

Molly and Mary Beth tried to sneak off without Tracy, but when they left they could see her down the street.

She was coming toward them.

She was pulling a big red wagon.

On the side of it, it said HELP A PET.

"We can put all the stuff in this," she called.

Molly and Mary Beth each had a big bag. They had not thought to bring a wagon.

"You can't get much in those bags," said Tracy. "Let's go down to Lake Street, where all the big houses are."

The girls followed Tracy.

Rat's knees! thought Molly. Tracy always gets her own way.

*　　*　　*

At the first house, the lady had no rummage to donate.

At the next house, no one was home.

But at the big white house on the corner, the lady said, "I like pets. I'll see what I can find."

The Scouts waited while the lady went into her closet.

She came out with five belts. And a sparkling necklace. Plus a bracelet with a blue stone in it.

"Thank you very much," said the Pee Wees.

"Do you think those are real diamonds?" asked Mary Beth, pointing to the necklace.

They watched the stones sparkle in the sun.

"We'll get a lot of money for the animal shelter if they are!" said Tracy. She wiped her nose with the back of her sleeve.

26

The girls collected more belts and jewelry. They collected some dresses and shoes. They even got some baby clothes at one house. One man gave them two winter coats.

People liked to help pets. The girls filled the whole wagon. The brown bags were filled up too. The bags were heavy.

"Set them in the wagon on top of the coats," said Tracy. "Then we can go to one more house."

"We've got enough," said Molly. "I'm hot. Let's go home."

Mary Beth wanted to go home too.

"Just one more house," said Tracy, sniffling. "This big one here with the rose garden."

The girls sighed. They followed Tracy up the walk to the door. On the door

was a sign that said:

DELIVERIES USE BACK DOOR.

"Is that us?" whispered Mary Beth.

"Not exactly," said Tracy.

28

But the girls trudged around to the back.

They rang the doorbell again and again.

Finally a man looked out the window.

He looked mean.

"We are collecting rummage," shouted Tracy. "To help pets."

"I don't like pets," said the man. "Go away."

"What a crab," muttered Molly. "A hex on that guy."

"We don't care," said Mary Beth. "We've got piles of stuff. We'll have more than anybody else."

The girls walked past the rose garden.

They walked down the sidewalk to where they had left the red wagon.

Then they stopped.

"Rat's knees!" said Molly. "Our wagon is gone!"

CHAPTER 5

The Red Wagon

Just then a big car drove by.

A girl was leaning out the window. "Hey!" she called out, and waved.

It was Rachel. Her mother was driving the car. It was filled with rummage for the sale.

"Have you seen a red wagon filled with rummage?" asked Tracy.

Rachel shook her head. Her mother drove off.

"I'll bet she took it," said Tracy.

"She didn't take it," said Mary Beth. "She has enough stuff of her own."

"It's your fault," grumbled Molly to Tracy. "You made us go to one more house."

The girls looked behind bushes and trees.

They looked to see if the wagon had rolled down the hill.

"It's gone," said Tracy. Her nose was really running now.

Yuck, thought Molly. But it was sad that Tracy had lost her wagon.

"Let's go tell Mrs. Peters what happened," said Mary Beth.

The girls walked slowly toward their leader's house.

They had no red wagon to pull.

They had no bags to carry.

They had no rummage to sell to help a pet.

*   *   *

When they got to Mrs. Peters's house, Rachel's car was in front. Rachel and her mother were carrying things into the garage for the sale.

"Hello!" called Mrs. Peters. "Did you come to help?"

Molly nodded. They could help sort the clothes. And put price tags on them.

"Why, just look at the carload of things that Rachel brought," Mrs. Peters said.

Molly looked.

A hex on Rachel. She always had to have the most of everything.

Even rummage.

"My goodness! Just look at the big load of things the boys are bringing," called Mrs. Peters from the doorway.

"What hardworking Pee Wees you boys are!" she said.

Molly turned around to look.

In the doorway stood Roger and Sonny and Tim.

Right beside them was Tracy's red wagon.

It was filled with coats and shoes and belts and jewelry!

CHAPTER 6
How Much Is That Doggy?

"Our diamonds!" shouted Tracy.

"Our belts and shoes and coats," said Mary Beth.

"You stole our rummage!" shouted Molly.

She wanted to go over and grab the diamonds out of Roger's hand.

She wanted to hit him. Smack, Smack, Smack!

She could too. She was strong.

But she didn't want to start a fistfight in Mrs. Peters's garage.

"This is our rummage," said Tim. "We found it sitting right on the sidewalk."

"It belongs to us!" shouted Tracy. "That's my wagon! And those are our diamonds."

"Prove it," said Roger. "I don't see your name on it."

All three girls talked at once. They told Mrs. Peters how they came out of the mean man's yard and found their wagon was gone.

"Nobody was near it," muttered Sonny. "How did we know it was yours?"

Tracy grabbed her red wagon back. She stuck her tongue out at the boys.

"The main thing is," said Mrs. Peters brightly, "that this rummage will help

36

the homeless pets. No matter whose it is!"

But it *did* matter, thought Molly.

We worked hard to get that rummage! Harder than Rachel.

Much, much harder than Roger, Tim, and Sonny.

The girls grumbled as they unloaded the wagon.

"What price should we put on the diamonds?" asked Mary Beth.

"We won't put a price on them," said Mrs. Peters. "We will sell them to the highest bidder. That way your necklace will bring in a lot of money for the shelter. It may not be made of real diamonds, but it is very pretty."

On the day of the sale, everyone was there.

All the Pee Wees.

All the parents.

All the neighbors.

HELP A PET, said a banner stretched across the top of the garage.

Tiny welcomed all the buyers with loud barks.

A sign in front of Mrs. Peters's house said, PEE WEE SCOUT SALE HERE TODAY! HELP A PET.

"Is he for sale?" asked one lady, pointing to Tiny.

"Oh, no," said Mrs. Peters. "He's my dog."

Molly had an idea! She leaned over and whispered into Mrs. Peters's ear.

Mrs. Peters grinned. "I think that's a wonderful idea, Molly," she said.

Then Mrs. Peters and Molly got into her car.

"We'll be right back," they called.

They drove to the animal shelter.

*   *   *

When they returned, Miss Penn was in the car. So were six cages, with a dog in each one!

"Kevin," called Mrs. Peters. "Could you boys help us with these?"

Roger and Sonny grabbed one cage.

Kevin and Tim grabbed another.

They lined them up in front of the garage.

"It looks like this is the animal shelter!" yelled Roger.

"Or a pet shop," said Sonny.

The people who came to buy rummage had to walk past the cages first.

"A dog sale to help dogs!" said Tim.

"It was Molly's idea," said Mrs. Peters.

"A super idea," Miss Penn agreed.

"We can find some good homes for the dogs and earn money for the shelter at the same time," Roger said.

CHAPTER 7

A Thousand Dollars for the Dogs

By noon, all the dogs were sold except one.

"They are going like hotcakes," said Miss Penn. "I'll go back and get some more. And I'll bring a cat or two."

"That was really smart," said Mary Beth to Molly. "How did you ever think of that?"

"When the lady wanted to buy Tiny," Molly explained. "She gave me the idea that we could sell dogs."

"Dogs make good rummage," said Mrs. Peters, smiling. "Molly is our Pee Wee hero today."

"I could have thought of that," said Rachel. "It's not so great."

"You're just jealous," said Tracy.

"Rachel's jealous, Rachel's jealous!" sang Sonny and Roger and Tim all together.

It was very crowded at the sale. All the rummage was selling quickly. There were just a few things left.

"Now," said Mrs. Peters. "I would like your attention please! It is time to bid for the necklace. Who can give us the largest bid to help the animal shelter?"

She held the necklace up in front of the crowd. It sparkled and glittered in the bright sun.

"The diamonds may not be real, but they are very pretty," Mrs. Peters said.

She began to read the bids that people
had written on pieces of paper. "Ten dollars from Mrs. Dolan," she read.

That seemed like a lot of money to
Molly.

"Twenty-five dollars from Joe Smithly," said Mrs. Peters.

Everyone cheered.

"Wow," said Lisa. "He must be rich."

Mrs. Peters kept reading off numbers and names. There were many bids in the box. Then all of a sudden she looked very surprised. "One thousand dollars!" she called.

"Ooh, aah," everyone said.

Who would bid one thousand dollars at a rummage sale?

The Pee Wee Scouts looked around.

"It's not my mom," said Lisa. "She doesn't have that much money."

"My mom does," said Rachel. "My dad's a dentist."

Rachel was always bragging about her dad, thought Molly.

The Pee Wees ignored Rachel.

"It must be a movie star," said Sonny.

Finally Mrs. Peters read the name on the paper. "Mrs. Noble," she said.

The Scouts looked all around. They tried to see if Mrs. Noble looked like a movie star.

"She'll have lots of makeup on her face," whispered Sonny.

"And gold rings on her fingers," said Tracy.

"Here I am!" called out a lady at the back of the crowd. "I'm Mrs. Noble."

But this lady did not have makeup on.

She did not wear gold rings. She had jeans on. And an old blue sweater.

"She's no movie star," scoffed Roger.

When she came closer, Tracy said, "Do you know who that is? That's the lady who gave us the necklace."

Molly looked. Rat's knees! Tracy was

right. Why would a lady pay one thousand dollars for her own necklace?

Mrs. Noble gave Mrs. Peters a check. Then she took the necklace. With a big smile on her face, she looked out into the crowd at Molly and Tracy and Mary Beth.

"When these nice girls came to my house," she said, "I was in such a hurry that I didn't realize I had given them my real diamond necklace."

Mrs. Peters's eyes opened wide. "Those were real diamonds in your wagon," she said.

"I knew that," said Molly.

"So did we," said Tracy and Mary Beth.

"The necklace is worth over ten thousand dollars," Mrs. Noble said with a smile.

Kevin whistled through his teeth.

"She is as rich as a movie star," said Tim. "Even if she isn't one."

"You could buy a house with ten thousand dollars. Or at least a sports car!" shouted Roger.

"It isn't just the money," said Mrs. Noble. "This necklace has been in my family a long time. I'm very glad to have it back. And I'm glad to donate this money to the animal shelter too."

Miss Penn went right up to the front of the crowd. "With this money," she said, "we can put in some new kennels with outdoor runs. Plus, we'll be able to take in more poor homeless dogs and cats for people to adopt. Thank you very much."

She shook Mrs. Noble's hand.

Mrs. Noble has pretty good rummage,

thought Molly. Thank goodness she and Mary Beth had gone along with bossy, drippy Tracy! If they hadn't, they would never have gone to Lake Street or to Mrs. Noble's house.

Maybe it wasn't so bad to be bossy after all.

At least when it's for a good cause.

CHAPTER 8

Leftover Puppy

That night the Pee Wee Scouts fell into bed. They were very hot. They were very tired. Molly was too tired even to eat supper. She slept like a rock.

But the next morning there was work to be done.

The Scouts rushed over to Mrs. Peters's house when they got up.

"I'll rake!" shouted Roger.

"I'll clean the garage," said Molly.

"I'll help Molly," said Mary Beth.

Sonny and I will pack up the leftover rummage," said Tim.

"Yeah," said Sonny. "We'll do it together."

All of the Scouts pitched in to help.

"Many hands make light work, my mom says," said Rachel.

By noon the yard was swept and cleaned.

Mrs. Peters poured some lemonade. It was another hot day.

"Yum," said Molly. She rubbed her stomach.

"Now," said Mrs. Peters, sitting down at the picnic table. "I want to congratulate Troop 23. You brought lots of money to the animal shelter. You brought more than any other Scout troop. But the best thing is, you all worked very hard. You did what Pee Wee Scouts should do. You helped others."

Molly was proud. She felt like bursting her buttons. Being a Scout made her feel good. Even if she didn't get a badge for it.

"We have only one thing to take care of," said Mrs. Peters.

"I know!" shouted Kevin. "The left-over puppy!"

The Pee Wees all looked at the one cage beside the driveway. Next to the cage sat one leftover puppy. All the others had been sold. Mrs. Peters had fed him and kept him in her house overnight.

Sonny brought the puppy some fresh water.

He patted him on the head.

Sonny was not afraid of puppies.

Only large dogs.

"We can't send him back," said Molly.

"Mrs. Peters, do we have to send this puppy back to the pound?" asked Tim.

"Well," said Mrs. Peters, pouring more lemonade for the Scouts, "we could use a mascot for Troop 23."

"Where would he live?" asked Molly, hoping it would be her house.

"We'll have to see if your mothers

would take turns keeping him," replied Mrs. Peters.

Tracy looked doubtful. She sneezed, loudly.

"Not Tracy's mom," added Mrs. Peters.

"Yeah!" the Scouts cheered. They all wanted a Pee Wee mascot. He was black with white feet. All the mothers will want him, thought Molly.

"Let's call him Spot," said Lisa.

"There are lots of better names than Spot," scoffed Rachel.

Lisa looked hurt.

"I like Paws," said Tracy.

"King," said Roger.

"Prince," said Kevin.

Mrs. Peters frowned. "Those are all good names," she said. "But if we do keep him, I think we should call him Lucky because he was lucky to be at a sale to help pets."

Troop 23 clapped loudly.

Some of the boys whistled.

Lucky was the best name for a maybe-mascot.

"This week," said Mrs. Peters, "I will call your mothers. If they agree to take turns keeping Lucky, we will have a mascot. I will let you know at our next meeting."

The Pee Wees groaned. It was a long time to wait.

Roger snapped a leash on Lucky's collar and took him for a run. Then everyone petted him. He tried to lick their hands. He wagged his tail.

"Lucky just has to be our mascot," said Mary Beth.

"He'll be a spoiled one," said Mrs. Peters, smiling.

"Why will he spoil?" said Tracy. She frowned.

The Scouts laughed.

"I mean he will get too much attention," said Mrs. Peters. "Not spoil like
food. If we keep him," she added.

Even though it was not a meeting, the
Scouts joined hands and sang their Scout

song. Then they said their Pee Wee Scout pledge.

Mrs. Peters looked pleased. Her troop had worked hard.

Harder than any other troop.

"Next week we will have new badges for you," she said.

The Scouts cheered at the news. They gave Lucky one last hug, and started home.

Molly felt good all over. They had worked hard. They would get new badges. They had helped homeless animals.

And maybe, just maybe, they would get a troop mascot.

CHAPTER 9

Mrs. Peters's Surprise

At last it was time for another meeting of the Pee Wees. Molly was eager to find out if the other mothers would agree to keep Lucky. Her mother had said yes.

Molly was excited about something else too. The Scouts had a surprise for Mrs. Peters.

During the week they had decided to give Mrs. Peters an end-of-the-summer thank-you party. Mrs. Peters had worked hard too.

Molly's mother made a huge cake.

Molly made a dog out of colored icing for the top. She gave the dog white paws. And a blue ribbon around his neck. A tag on the ribbon said LUCKY in little letters.

Sonny's mother sent potato salad from the deli. "Because she works," said Sonny proudly. "Otherwise she would have made it herself, she said."

Rachel's mother made little bitty sandwiches in the shape of dogs and cats. They had cream cheese and olives in them. Some had anchovies.

"Yuck," said Roger when he tasted one. He spit the anchovy out.

Rachel sighed. "My mother said she thought that might happen," Rachel told them. "She said some children might not know what anchovies were, if they didn't go to parties often."

Roger stuck out his tongue at her. He

brought hot dogs. His mother called them perfectly good-tasting hot dogs.

Tracy brought soda pop. "Allergy-free," she said. "It has no preservatives in it."

The Pee Wees couldn't wait to surprise Mrs. Peters. They snuck the food in the back door while some of the Pee Wees went to the front.

They tied balloons to the chairs.

They put the food on the table.

When Mrs. Peters came into the kitchen, they all yelled, "SURPRISE!"

Tiny and Lucky both began to bark.

"How exciting!" cried Mrs. Peters. "Oh, my goodness! What a nice way to end the dog days of August."

"Dog days?" said Kevin.

"The end-of-summer days in August are called dog days," Mrs. Peters explained. "When there is green algae on the lake and you can't swim."

61

Lucky howled at her words. Owoooo!

"We have our own dog days," said Molly. "We have had dog days the whole Help-a-Pet month!"

Everyone laughed and got in line behind Mrs. Peters for food.

Then their leader had badges to give out to the Scouts for working so hard at the rummage sale to help a pet. The Pee Wees pinned them on their shirts.

"Our troop surely helped pets more than any other troop!" said Mrs. Peters proudly.

The Scouts could not wait any longer.

"Do we have a mascot?" shouted Roger.

"Can we keep Lucky?" asked Molly.

Mrs. Peters smiled. The Scouts did not move.

"Yes!" she said. "There were enough mothers who could take turns keeping Lucky. So he is our new mascot."

Lucky barked a high puppy bark. Yip! Yip!

Tiny barked a low bark. Arf! Arf!

And Troop 23 cheered loudly. "Yeah!" they shouted. "He is ours!"

"And now," Mrs. Peters went on, "I have another little surprise for you."

The Scouts looked up at their leader.

What kind of a surprise? Molly wondered.

They had their new badges.

They had a Scout mascot.

What kind of a surprise could it be?

The Pee Wees sat on the floor in a big circle. Mrs. Peters sat in a chair. She smiled at the Scouts. Then she said, "My surprise is some big news. I am going to have a little Pee Wee Scout of my own. In a few months I am going to have a baby!"

The Pee Wees were very quiet. Molly

felt shocked. She had never thought of Mrs. Peters with a baby of her own. She was their Scout leader. She wasn't a mother.

Some of the Pee Wees looked at each other.

We should say we are happy, thought Molly. But instead Molly wanted to say, Will you still be our leader?

No one said anything. They just sat and looked at Mrs. Peters.

Then Roger whispered to Molly, "Babies can't be Scouts."

"I know you are all surprised," Mrs. Peters went on. "But I will still be your Scout leader. Our troop will still meet here every Tuesday. We will just have one more little Scout at our meetings."

"Yeah!" shouted Molly.

Then all the Pee Wees cheered.

The boys ran up and shook Mrs. Peters's hand. The girls gave her little hugs.

Then, when Mr. Peters came home, they cheered for him too.

A baby might be fun, thought Molly. She didn't have any little brothers or sisters.

"Maybe we can take it for a walk in a stroller," said Mary Beth.

Mary Beth was very motherly, thought Molly.

"My mom will buy it a real cute dress if it's a girl," said Rachel.

"I hope it doesn't have allergies," said Tracy, wiping her nose.

It was time for the surprise party to end.

They had come to give Mrs. Peters a surprise. And instead, she gave one to them!

The Pee Wees got into a circle. They held hands.

First they said the Pee Wee Scout pledge together. Then they sang the Pee Wee Scout song.

Suddenly Molly felt a good feeling in the bottom of her stomach. It felt like her birthday or Christmas. But it wasn't.

"Rat's knees!" she said. "I love Pee Wee Scouts!"

Pee Wee Scout Song

(to the tune of
"Old MacDonald Had a Farm")

Scouts are helpers, Scouts have fun,
Pee Wee, Pee Wee Scouts!
We sing and play when work is done,
Pee Wee, Pee Wee Scouts!

With a good deed here,
And an errand there,
Here a hand, there a hand,
Everywhere a good hand.

Scouts are helpers, Scouts have fun,
Pee Wee, Pee Wee Scouts!

Pee Wee Scout Pledge

We love our country
And our home,
Our school and neighbors too.

As Pee Wee Scouts
We pledge our best
In everything we do.